Amy Loves the Rain

by Julia Hoban

pictures by Lillian Hoban

Harper & Row, Publishers

For Elizabeth

Amy Loves the Rain
Text copyright © 1989 by Julia Hoban
Illustrations copyright © 1989 by Lillian Hoban
Printed in Singapore. All rights reserved.

Library of Congress Cataloging-in-Publication Data
Hoban, Julia.
 Amy loves the rain.

 Summary: Amy and her mother drive through the rain to
pick up Daddy.
 [1. Rain and rainfall—Fiction. 2. Parent and
child—Fiction] I. Hoban, Lillian, ill. II. Title
PZ7.H63487Af 1989   [E]   87-45851
ISBN 0-06-022357-X
ISBN 0-06-022358-8 (lib. bdg.)

1 2 3 4 5 6 7 8 9 10
First Edition

Amy Loves the Rain

It is a rainy day.
Amy sits in her car seat.

Let's pick up Daddy, Amy,
so he doesn't have to walk in the rain.

It is warm in the car on a rainy day.

The windshield wipers go *swish swak*.

The raindrops patter *pit pat*.

The car goes through a puddle—*splash plash*.

The sky is gray.

The streets are black and shiny.

The traffic light shines in the puddles.
Bright red, bright green.

Look, there is a man with a big umbrella.

Amy has an umbrella too.

Does Daddy have an umbrella?

No, he forgot his.

Daddy holds a newspaper over his head.

Amy, give Daddy your umbrella,

and he will give you a hug.